BITTER ANGEL

POEMS BY

AMY GERSTLER

NORTH POINT PRESS
San Francisco 1990

Some of these poems appeared in the following
magazines and anthologies: *B-City, Best American
Poetry, Blind Date, Columbia Magazine, Deep
Down: New Sensual Writing by Women, Enclitic, Fire
over Water, Frank, The L.A.I.C.A. Journal, Lemon
Fingers, New American Writing, Ouija Madness, Paris
Review, Poetry Loves Poetry: An Anthology of Los
Angeles Poets, Santa Monica Review, Up Late:
American Poetry Since 1970*, and *Witness*.

In "Della's Modesty" the quotations in italics were
culled from three novels by Erle Stanley Gardner: *The
Case of the Dangerous Dowager, The Case of the
Postponed Murder*, and *The Case of the Fenced in
Woman*.

The following people are gratefully acknowledged for
their help and support: Dennis Cooper, Tina Gerstler,
Michelle Huneven, James and Nancy Krusoe, Jennie
McDonald, Kate Moses, Jack Shoemaker, Robert
Tomlinson, David Trinidad, Benjamin Weissman, and
Megan Williams.

LIBRARY OF CONGRESS
CATALOGING-IN-PUBLICATION DATA
Gerstler, Amy.
  Bitter angel : poems / by Amy Gerstler.
    p.   cm.
  ISBN 0-86547-408-7
  I. Title.
PS3557.E735B58   1990
811'.54—dc20   89-16083

North Point Press
850 Talbot Avenue
Berkeley, California
94706

CONTENTS

"Let me try to put it for you in a nutshell. In life we shall live together; in death we shall mingle our dust. How will that do?"

Bao-yu, in Cao Xueqin's
The Story of the Stone

BITTER ANGEL

SIREN

I have a fish's tail, so I'm not qualified to love you.
But I do. Pale as an August sky, pale as flour milled
a thousand times, pale as the icebergs I have never seen,
and twice as numb—my skin is such a contrast to the rough
rocks I lie on, that from far away it looks like I'm a baby
riding a dinosaur. The turn of centuries or the turn
of a page means the same to me, little or nothing.
I have teeth in places you'd never suspect. Come. Kiss me
and die soon. I slap my tail in the shallows—which is to say
I appreciate nature. You see my sisters and me perched
on rocks and tiny islands here and there for miles:
untangling our hair with our fingers, eating seaweed.

CLAIRVOYANCE

I've an uncommon calling.
I was born without immunity
to this din in the air:
the sad humming of the long lost.
Imagine not being able
to help hearing every word
that's been moaned in this kitchen
for the last thousand years,
and random sounds too, from snorting
in the stable that stood here
before your house was built,
to the croakers' whisperings
at the bottom of the pond
which filled this hollow before that,
when this county was all swamp. The song
of every being that passed through here
still echoes and is amplified in me.
The sour spirits of the drowned
who imbibed brackish water
remain huddled here, dripping,
in your kitchen. Mouth to mouth
they resuscitate themselves
and speak, lip-syncing twice-baptized cries
an ironclad silence now surrounds.
They're hemmed in, like we are, on all sides . . .
Chastity and impatience keep us from each other;
the barbed wire of gossip, catholicism
and obstinacy all come between us.
But we can still do something about it.
Think of the poor ghosts,
with no pleasures left, except watching us.
Let's keep them amused. It's all we can offer.

—

4

I'm begging now, like those ghosts
who no longer know any better,
who often entreat me to trespass
outside the confines of my slight
power. I don't know how else to ask:
I want to have you to ponder
when I join their damp precincts.

Somewhere under the weather
snores our drugged hero:
a gladiator or astronaut,
lying in a fringed hammock
in his mother's garden,
waiting to be wakened
and loosed upon the world.
Quick, into my arms before
the next tremor hits.
Just beneath these monsoons,
an aurora borealis trembles.
Tucked into its luminous
gunbelt, a change of luck,
an abrupt windfall tunes up,
just for us. Soon,
instead of zinging bullets
we'll find ourselves drenched
in concertos. I have no
authority to comfort
you, though I try.
If all this is to vanish,
if you and I are lost,
set loose, wounded,
to wander among uncomplaining
trees, fingering their lightly
haired, sticky little leaves,
then hand me my camera.
I must take pictures.

In this picture, a well-read young mother ponders a paragraph in a magazine on her lap while her child naps. An article called "The Riddle of Illness." Dry winds blow germs into the nursery by the millions. Window screens only sift them. They elude disinfectant and bloom in room-temperature air, so much more hospitable than the elements. A few germs float up the baby's nose while the mother reads, making the infant sneeze. Under the microscope, viruses look like corkscrew noodles, or other varieties of pasta, waving hairy little legs. *The earlier a syndrome is diagnosed, the quicker we as parents can face facts and make intelligent decisions. The waiver allows your physician to do whatever he deems necessary.* If she stuffs the baby's ears with sanitary cotton wads, it will miss Al Green, romantic maniac, yodeling and pleading, in sweet falsetto from the radio, *Call me.* The baby's eyes pop open. It seems to see the swarming pests, much tinier than any flyswatter's mesh, that teem between floor and ceiling. Delighted, the baby laughs, its giggle a sound from another planet. It wiggles sticky fingers and rubs its curled feet together, elated, then sober the next second, as it figures out how each wriggle or blurt is chased by its reciprocal: a barren sadness . . . the wake left by every gesture.

DOUBT

It's a fat cactus
desert travelers tap
for a mucuslike lubricant
that protects their skins.
It's the psyche's dry lakebed
from which moans of pleasure
bubble up in gaseous form
and crack the sunbaked mud.
How should I know what moves you—
who shivers in your distance,
a prostrate mirage on the cheap
green bedspread in the only
air-conditioned motel in town—
the one with the hole punched
through the bathroom door?
You're afraid of your own thoughts.
You keep staring at the sky,
where one magnificent fleecy doubt,
several miles in diameter hovers,
just above that spot on the horizon
also known as the vanishing point . . .
where the sun begins to burn off
all you ever held dear.

In Bible times heavenly messengers disguised as beggars were everywhere. Divine communiqués arrive nowadays via strange mediums. Meanings profuse and profound are inscribed in everyday life's most minor designs: the way glasses and plates rearranged themselves when our backs were turned, how my sisters and I seemed to read each other's minds, and times when something in the attic groaned at such appropriate moments. These were glimmers, little inklings, of what we longed for. At times, from our window, we'd watch homeless men skulk around our yard, exhibiting big discrepancies between their teeth. Father would send them away. But those poor prevented messengers! How could Father have known the effects his protections would have on four daughters, stuck in this small town few people ever leave? High hopes deteriorate here like houseboats sunk into mud at the bottom of an ancient Chinese waterway. We offer God strict, intimate prayers, but perhaps it would be better to simply admit our helplessness and send up waves of that agony instead. The homeless men paced under our windows at dusk, sometimes singing a little—"River Jordan is deep and wide / Milk and honey on the other side." Those lyrics, in earthy baritones, sung by shirtless sweating men, seemed to beckon us toward unchristian vistas. Something in the thirsty way they mouthed the word "milk" made me want to jump down from our window, into their midst, though it was some distance. These were sooty, threatening men, wearing huge weathered boots. Men with cabbage or worse on their breaths. Men on whom all clothing looked baggy and unnatural. Men who washed by sloshing trough-water on their chests and upper arms. We girls pined to be pinned down by something heavy and gruff. One of us would sometimes rub her cheek against a tree trunk, scraping her skin on its bark. There was one man in particular, less well built than the others. At noon I caught sight of him bending down, across the meadow. When he lifted his head, sunlight shone through his ears, giving them a red glow, and I remembered the blood in him. I could almost see his delicate, hairlike capillaries, and I thought about my downfall.

SHRINE

The house of her birth was pulled down,
having stood many years waiting
in patience for her return, which took
place not long afterwards. *Kiss the dust*
of the vacant lot. Reunite with it.
Preserve your solitude, the only holy
thing about you! She labored under
a false notion of the heroic.
She revered her teachers,
beside whose brilliance she felt
stumbling and stupid. Now that's my kind
of saint. The more neurotic, unattractive
and accident prone, the better.
The more easily redeemed. *When you*
finally recognize me, please kneel.

RISING UP

Last summer, god washed
his hands of me.
Scissors, nickels, noon,
radio, religion, whiskey:
all lost to me. No way
for you to know what shape
I'm in now. Of course it's me.
Remember, you stubbed your toe
in the kitchen and felt our
daughter in a distant city
fall and skin her knee?
You can't come after me.
My traits escaped in a blaze.
I ditched my dripping limbs
at the mouth of a splendid cave—
became intimate with the glittering
similarities between whirlpools
and the flow of human hair.
The dispossessed cool their heels
here a thousand years,
then disperse their gifts
downwards. Thump, thump.
Hunks of excess Christian
wisdom people perceive as hail
over the Appalachias.
My treasure lands in soft places:
the Feather River bed, tar pits
and the dent in your felt hat,
its crown worn out as your
welcome in that thistle-filled
valley.

That stand of trees at the edge of the meadow senses a sin is about to be committed in its midst, and the trees groan. Insects swarm in a dim whir of prediction. Nature in her radiance provides the following symbology: a snake glimpsed in a clearing means the reopening of an old wound. A sapling represents youth and enthusiasm. Spiderwebs signify estrangement. A natal plum is harbinger of a fresh start. Nimbus clouds equal confusion. In nature, in literature, the wind hints. Cows practically mouth syllables of the plot with their cud. A flash flood serves to underline a paragraph. The antics of wild animals provide irony.

I waited for your coming, and barely recognized you when you finally arrived. Now I await your return, though the snail, acacia, and flea assure me it won't take place in this lifetime. Magnolia leaves clatter to the asphalt, the prelude, I hope, to your approach. Birds tattle and snitch. Their predictions, while melodious, are overly optimistic.

The sun cuts us apart, as speech does. Darkness welds us back together, temporarily. Night pads the damage. Dawn comes up and shapes regain their edges. The main character wakes in mute panic and won't talk at all, or begins to babble immediately, even before coffee. This character takes a long walk and observes tall grasses still tremble, shrubs flower, and sap runs, regardless of his burgeoning inner turmoil.

The sacred grove, the burning bush, the magic circle. Signs some of us wait all our lives for. The fox that talks. The ant that spells out the answer, laboriously, in dried peas. *He's alright. He's not dead. He hasn't harmed himself or anyone else. That wasn't a gunshot you heard. He'll arrive home on the bus, sometime during the next decade.* Winter grass dries up. A path is revealed. Suddenly everything begins to look sinister. Ducks and geese abruptly take flight, quacking and honking. Ominous. Something has spooked them. A dog goes mad at noon in the dusty street. He's only a noun but nevertheless, the whole town follows suit. *Instead of a sweet smell*, the Bible says, *let there be stink.*

A field of wheat ripples and imparts little, its gestures attributed to wind. The sun makes our decisions, when the time is ripe. Fog rolls in. Waves break. We can't see much. The horizon's almost rubbed out.

From time to time, characters who revere nothing and feel nothing, save what nature presents and dispels, paw the ground. They throw themselves down, on the earth's composted mercy. They grasp at straws, branches or reeds . . . any of the plants that do such faithful service as images, passed from hand to hand, from ancestor to ancestor. The grapevine overtakes the gardenia. Parasites deplete their hosts. The unwatered lawn is distraught, and one oversensitive schoolboy imagines he can hear its parched blades whimpering.

It's what's behind me that I am . . . that remote portion of forest, within which a withered poplar blooms. That stand of trees will back me up.

What does the cedar tree seem to be saying? Even dust exhibits a countenance . . . such an old, pagan observation. Did Grandpa really will his soul to enter the oak sofa? At this point in the proceedings, the scenery makes a short speech. No more beating around the bush. The background was in a continual state of agitation then, much as it is today . . . germinating and wilting like crazy . . . you never knew when a hedge would become a cathedral, or a cathedral a sprig of jimsonweed.

EMBER DAYS

Dear Maker, I've failed.
Lost my tongue. Put words
back in my mouth again,
or blackberries maybe,
and concepts back in my
head. Lead me down
into your backyard
which never ceases,
with its apricots
and onyx, its green breath
and feces, being Eden.

IN PERPETUAL SPRING

Gardens are also good places
to sulk. You pass beds of
spiky voodoo lilies
and trip over the roots
of a sweet gum tree,
in search of medieval
plants whose leaves,
when they drop off
turn into birds
if they fall on land,
and colored carp if they
plop into water.

Suddenly the archetypal
human desire for peace
with every other species
wells up in you. *The lion
and the lamb cuddling up.*
The snake and the snail, kissing.
Even the prick of the thistle,
queen of the weeds, revives
your secret belief
in perpetual spring,
your faith that for every hurt
there is a leaf to cure it.

Miracle mongers. Bedwetters. Hair-shirted wonder workers. Shirkers of the soggy soggy earth. A bit touched, or wholly untouched living among us? They shrug their bodies off and waft with clouds of celestial perfume. No smooching for this crew, except for hems, and pictures of their mothers . . . their lips trespass only the very edges of succor. *Swarms of pious bees precede her.* One young girl wakes up with a ring on her finger and a hole in her throat. Another bled milk when her white thigh was punctured. All over the world, a few humans are born each decade with a great talent for suffering. They have gifts that enable them to sleep through their mistreatment: the sleep of the uncomplaining just, the sleep of the incomplete. Our relationship to them is the same as our relationship to trees: what they exhale, we breathe.

INNOCENCE

Maple trees' sugary
belief in the seasons.
The smirk that snakes
across the wooden buddha's
fat face, bragging he's
achieved a petrified peace.
The oak's elephantlike
benevolence as an angry
schoolboy carves surly
sentiments into the thick
skin of its trunk.
The verdict of acorns,
the unknowing mercy which
runs, medicinal-smelling,
through feverish leaves'
veins, while light blithely
manufactures more and more
of itself. Chlorophyll's
force, its unassailable
deep green justice
seeds forests everywhere,
via ashlike airborne spores.

Dung heap. Poor cooled shell.
Orange peel. Husk, crust, bark.
Armor my meat rode beneath—
stink-mobile with me asleep
at the wheel. Fleas' breeding
ground. Rigamarole of gristle
and digits. Pain parlor. Gate
left ajar. Walls of my old home;
I gaze back on you with disbelief:
How could you have kept me prisoner
for so long?

Cutlet carved from our larger carcasses:
thus were you made—from spit and a hug.
The scratchy stuff you're lying on is wool.
You recognize the pressure of your mother's hand.
That white moon with a bluish cast is a priest's face,
frowning over a water bowl. Whatever befalls you now,
you've been blessed, in a most picturesque
and ineffective ceremony dating from the Middle Ages.
Outdoors, the church lawn radiates a lethal green.
A gas truck thunders down the street.
Why, at emotional moments, do the placid trees
and landscape look overexposed, almost ready
to bleach away, and reveal the workings
of "the Real" machine underneath?
All bundled up on such a hot day:
whose whelp, pray tell, or mutton chop are you?
—tail-less, your cloudy gaze a vague accusation,
not of the sins of my history, but ignorance
to come, future cruelty. You're getting red
in the face, blotchy, ready to wail. Good.
From now on protest and remember everything.
Your cries assail even the indigent dead,
buried in charity plots right outside,
slowly releasing their heat, while you,
born out of the blue into a wheezing spring,
watch a chaotic mosaic assemble itself.
You tune up. My love for you is half adrenaline,
half gibberish. More Latin and the priest
splatters you. He's got one good eye,
and a black patch, like a pirate.
Now, smiling as if he knows something I don't,
he hands you to me. If I drop you, loudmouth,

will you bounce or fly? You were chalky
and bloody at first, in the doctor's grip,
looking skinned and inside-out.
Boyhood, a dangling carrot. I stare at you
and experience the embarrassment of riches. I
need to loosen my tie or I'll faint.
Outside a rake scrapes, sprinklers hiss.
It might be best to set you down
in one of these squares of light on the floor,
striped by venetian blinds, and leave you safe
in that bright cage. I could go have coffee,
and come back when we can carry on
a conversation. Men and women are afraid
of each other. It's true. Whisper
and drool of my flesh, I'm terrified of you.

This news is so bad it won't stay in your head. Every second you're afraid you'll forget it. You've always been a terrible messenger, a bumbler, a conduit for trouble. After your alarm about forgetting passes, you become afraid you'll laugh while trying to pronounce the words. You worry the same giggles that afflict you during the eulogy at funerals will seize you the minute you moisten your lips to speak. Then a more rigid panic grabs you. You're afraid the person you're telling this grim tale to will also begin to laugh, louder and louder, till his voice completely fills the room, and you can practically see the huge black HA HA HA's scrawled in the air, vibrating like violin strings, just as in cartoons. Eventually the other person will stop laughing and twist your head off.

Delivering awful news is like having to eat a knife, tearing the blade off in bites and chewing it up as if it were only a piece of the thin silver foil chocolate mints come wrapped in. Action slows down to a crawl. It seems you're suddenly underwater. You walked down the hall under your own power and stuck your head into your father's study. But because of what you saw, a current clumsily ushers you back into the kitchen, where your mother's unloading groceries, a can of stewed tomatoes in each hand. Your mouth opens and closes like a sea creature's, but no plankton swim in. She says, "what's wrong?" Then centuries go by: a blur of summerfallwinterspringsummerswintersfalls. Leaves color, shrivel, and plummet to the ground. Branches bud, and the flowers gape and drop off. . . over and over. All in the space of the eight seconds it takes you to answer your mother. This is why it's said tragedy ages you prematurely. It causes the little movie of your life to run through the projector at fast forward till you can get the right words out of your mouth and stop the runaway film. You want to believe you saw wrong. Maybe you only dreamed you poked your head into Dad's study and his slumped body with its head and hands on the messy desk had its back to you. You dreamed you tiptoed up from behind and read the note on the blotter in his well-tailored handwriting. The problem is, you're wide awake as you take the canned tomatoes out of your mother's hands and set them on the counter next to the toaster. Then you pull her down the hall by her sleeve.

You force her into your dream. You stop short of the door, and point, so she has to push you, gently, out of the way. "I haven't got time for your shenanigans," she says briskly. When she enters, nothing happens for a few seconds, but you know she sees, because she sags a little, knees buckling slightly, as though a huge hand had dropped her there from a great height. She puts her arms around him from behind and one of his arms falls off the desk and dangles like a doll's. Then she lays her head on his and closes her eyes. This is your fault. You led her right to it.

If you slip out into the backyard after the cars start pulling up, no one will notice your absence. Your mother answers terrible questions, bears everything—the clumping boots muddying the carpet, interrupting voices, the constant use of the phone. A committee of neighbors is out on the lawn, consulting each other. Maybe they're shading their eyes.

There are blinding bright patches and dead cold spots in the air, and whatever light's there buries you. When it gets dark, a long slow fuse is lit in you by the stars. You smolder and feel you're dissolving, like the contents of some sarcophagus thousands of years old that's been dug up by grave robbers. You're nothing but a mummy who's been preserved inside four elaborate airtight coffins, the innermost of which is covered with writing—every sacred phrase your dead language ever possessed. The overeager, sweat-drenched marauders don't wait till they get back to the hideout. They pry open your box right then and there. Your bones turn to dust instantaneously, as soon as the air hits them. But your reduction to dust provides no moment of clemency, no flash in which you are vaporized so your residue can mingle with the mineral elements. Consciousness takes many forms, all of them obstinate. Ground to powder (for the first or your trillionth time?), the hieroglyphics composed specifically for you still sing of the long and difficult journey you must make in utter darkness to have your heart weighed.

We inhabited an ecstatic landscape—
in winter quintessentially bare,
in spring visited by storms bright
and violent as operas. You promised
you wouldn't burn out first—not in words,
but with grunts, mutters, facial tics
and cryptic postscripts. Yet a melody
came that spirited you away—you always
were a sucker for contagious tunes.
During the years I drank and drank
your advantage, I was rapt.
The outside world could jabber
and clang, wreak deep brown and purple
havoc . . . but I was right with you,
panting to keep up, in fact. Arias,
monologues, yelps, and dead letters:
perhaps they began to sound munched
and unintelligible. Yet you were
perpetually worth listening to, as you
struggled to fight free of false euphorias
and respiratory crisis. Sink or swim,
rain or shine, I wished, and sometimes
still dream, that in your sleep,
by some sweet means, you turn toward me.

The window's wide open.
The crowns of a blue-leafed
and a green-leafed tree
are visible outdoors, in front
of a ridge of washed-out mountains.
Propped up on one elbow,
leaning his cheek on his hand,
he looks at her as she sleeps,
facing away from him. She lies
with her head on her crooked arm.
A blue blanket seeps from between
her knees. Their bed fills the room,
looking less like a bed
than a small stage.
The thin mattress doesn't seem
to rest on anything.
The third figure on the bed's
a brown dog, his tame face
resting on crossed paws.
He's also fast asleep.
Both humans are naked.
The man's skin is so much darker
than the woman's, he seems
to belong to a different race.
The sight of her white form
won't leave him in peace.
When he shuts his eyes,
her aura flares on his retinas:
a fuzzy brightness he finds
himself tender custodian of.
If it were to vanish,
he'd feel like a blind man,

chasing the irreplaceable.
He thinks he would disappear.
As it is, his attentions
have little to lean on.
Still, they wind themselves
around the rickety trellis
of her skeleton. One must
restrain one's love.
One mustn't act as though
waking up in the morning
is some kind of breakthrough,
a marvelous accomplishment,
an occasion for cake
and champagne, though in fact,
it is. Among all our joys,
he thinks, it is the setting
of that last persistent star,
right before morning,
that stands out.

Believing it will be, so shall it be!
A group of English mystics, in a time
not far distant, swam the lapping grey channel.
Their bodies greased head to toe,
rubber caps with ear flaps hiding
scant hair, they felt no cold.
Arms parting the waves, they contemplated:
    the love of the plow for the furrow,
    the musician's love of his rendition,
    the bracelet's love of its wrist,
    the masochist's reaction to the kiss
    of the whip, how newborns adore forceps,
and many other complicated loves,
the dimmest of which the swimming
mystics mentally translated into Latin
and other dead languages when the chill
began to get the upper hand, threatening
to douse their personal researches.
The dignity of labor, the uses of chloroform,
contrasts in morality during prosperity
versus plaguetime, arousal and wretchedness,
and the sleep of disappointed spinsters
were all called to mind, till the narrow
channel teemed with thoughts so concrete
the sea seemed crowded with schools
of some silvery but gill-less
form of fish, and each sage, musing to
the rhythm of his waterlogged crawl,
was seized by a sensation that, attuned at last

to this channel's weak current, he could
stretch out his hand and grab a piece
of the big idea they were all swimming
in, as it passed from mind to mind.
Of course they all drowned. Even me.

Malign my character, but do it under a willow,
with my ready-made mourner already bent at the waist.

Listen, peabrain, you have influence. Use it.
Do as I say. Start by kneeling. Tell him you're sorry
and you'll never do it again. Get him to spit out his gum and pay
    attention.
It's easy. Kiss him as if you're a little bit thirsty.

I was patiently waiting for you to explain these flowering phenomena.
Now I might as well be a prehistoric ear of corn, so ancient its kernels
are working loose, like some old geezer's teeth.

Birds nest on the shores of a secluded lake.
Reptiles and waterfowl that populate the swamp watched
the skiff drift downriver, guided by the current.

The pastor receives letters from parishioners that pose
questions about heaven: 1. Will we be conscious
of the world's continuance? 2. Will we be cognizant
of those loved ones left behind?

"You go on ahead. I'll be out in a minute,"
she had said at the back door. She hated to think
they'd come all this way for nothing, so she went
upstairs, to have herself one last look.

DISPERSION

Restored to me via the glossy homicide
of photographs, I examine your face.
A map of Jerusalem, holy and dangerous.
Your mouth and brow—epithets I'm not sure
I deserve. Your hands perfect, inedible
sugar birds, perched atop a saint's
name-day cake. Your gaze an edict
I can no longer follow.

I longed to please you more
than any inner heathen or priest.
How fiercely I miss your vicinity—
your thoughts charged and dark
as breezes that brave mausoleums.

Though you've removed yourself
from the greedy reach of my five senses,
I put my ear to any ground now—
drenched or parched, planted or fallow,
and from this minute till doomsday,
I'll hear you. Parts of my skeleton
were formed just to conduct the sounds
of your footfall. That slight vibration
sets my most delicate bones in motion.
When you put your foot down, it resounds
faintly, like a dozen harps left standing
on a windy hill. If I listen intently,
nothing can muffle those notes of amnesty.
Even you can't sever that kind of connection.

APPROACH

How could I lose sight of him? I only know that my eyes followed him as far as possible, till my gaze wandered over the horizon's brink, where insight and blindness alike are insufficient. When I go for a walk in the afternoon to mail letters, avoiding my own eyes in windows or water, I frequently have the feeling I'm just about to see him. When I get into bed at night, all bundled up, the bedclothes exhale a whiff reminiscent of him, though he's never set foot in this room. Tonight I click off the light and lie on my back, my hands behind my head as though I were lying in wet grass, waiting for rabbits and deer to leap over me, or something heavier to puncture my stomach with its hoof. I wait for my eyes to adjust to the darkness, then for the night birds to begin sounding off. I think about him for what seems like a long time, and about how sad it is that what I jot down daily, or mull over in the walled chamber behind my eyes, can't hold a candle to his flickering image, can't show me some fresh vision of him, or explain why I constantly feel, as I drift off, that he's watching me.

Say it. Spell it out. Confess. Let loose. Trees thrust up, and the earth cracks so they can. Streams weep. Oceans roar. Why shouldn't they undamn themselves and speak? And why shouldn't we? Anoint me with your voice, its flat twang. God's voice breaks cedars, our voices just break. His tongue reaches from one end of the earth to the other. *There is but one master, broken into as many fragments as there are motes of dust.* And the first twenty-six of those fragments, my love, are our alphabet.

We're afraid of forgetting what we've seen, so we write it down and black characters wriggle nervously from the pen nib. Then the ink dries and conveys, at best, a state of consciousness similar to the one created by music. Or at worst, some gibberish coughed up in a weak moment. *Honey, I can hear a man puking his guts out in the backyard again. Will you please go and see who it is?*

Blessed is he no one can comprehend, know, meditate on, or make an object of thought. Blessed is he known only through his works, for he is safe from slander, and the mystery of the alphabet hovers above his head and protects him like a cloud of stinging insects.

Sages say: Study *The Book of Splendor* and *The Encyclopedia of Radiance.* Personally, the *Guide to the Perplexed* has long been my favorite volume.

Blessed is he who guided me here. But why has he now made himself impossible to follow? Such a steep ascent. . . I can't keep up with him. And the falling snow quickly fills in his footprints.

What's missing from this picture? The sound of flutes that heralds the dissolution of cities. There, there, my cherry, guava, plum. I can't think of any more sweet names for you that won't rot your teeth. Don't cry. Our surroundings just tumbled down around our ears when the trumpet sounded, that's all.

On a public elevator, begin your long song cycle. Between the first and second floors, sing of the sleepwalker about to step off a cliff. Between the tenth and eleventh floors, give voice to the solitary insomniac staring at the moon as he picks loose threads from his bedclothes. In a year he'll have completely unraveled. As the elevator climbs higher, up to the twenty-seventh floor, sing of the young girl who smoked opium for the first time and cried out: "Oh I am an angel!"

"Delight at the beginning and bitterness at the end" was mother's description of guess what: sex. But everyone heard that when they were young. That sentence has always been used against us.

So what's it like for you? I'm all ears, really. Does the pleasure of entry become a lie the second you're inside? At first you don't know where you are: that's the heaven you'd hoped for. But then you're bumping against the walls again and her face floats back into focus, always the same. There's no word for this particular disappointment. And the love-blather she demands at such times is distracting. The sound of your own voice, always hoarse at such moments, sets matters straight, just when you most need them to remain aslant and strange. Then she starts talking. "Whoa, boy. Slow down. Hold on a second . . ." and the sounds she mouths ruin everything.

Sometimes he takes the blame in his arms and cuddles it, and sometimes he calls it down directly upon his head, but it never splatters him. He's an immaculate man.

Worms are found only in sweet things. A man killed his neighbor and buried the body beneath his fig tree but the figs grew so sweet that the murderer was found out.

In *As You Like It*, while dressed as a man, Rosalind admonishes Orlando: "Men have died, and worms have eaten them, but not for love." Throughout the play, she wears a ring with the word "drunkenness" engraved on it to remind her of certain vows she made to herself.

I can feel the strands of my spirit unbraiding, because after all is said and felt, I still love him. I'm coming undone. Why does it always have to be midnight? Beside my bed is a water clock. Hear it drip and chime? When we were together, he was the chime and I the drip. When the time comes, why must it be midnight, so I'm left straddling the fence again between the departing day and the coming one?

I love you. Your smell is the smell of a field the rain has blessed. You're the fountain and I'm the parched dust pigeons and sparrows flick over their wings when the fountain is dry. My mother watched birds doing this and said they were giving themselves a "dust bath." She used so many wonderful expressions.

Take that out of your mouth. Can't you taste that it's bad for you? Have you lost all connection with nature, all instinct? Nothing natural tastes *that* sweet. Spit it out into my hand and I'll throw it away.

Twigs shooting forth from an ancient branch. In other words, I had to endure the annoying chatter of an old man. I wanted to remain quiet. He bothered me with every kind of foolish question. Kept pestering me the whole trip. It would have been enough just to have to look at his face, folding and crinkling itself from one expression into another.

She discloses her secrets only to those that love her. She wanted to lie down and dally among the grass and wild plants. This is no time for sleeping, he said. And you have burrs stuck to your butt, he reproached her, looking disgusted. Might another man have found her rustic abandon charming? She's a rose before intercourse and a lily afterwards. She left despite all my pleading. No note, no postcard. Not a word from her since. I want all this to mean something. My ears strain the warm darkness for sounds. This silence of hers must be some kind of code and I will decipher it.

No one has much patience these days.
There's precious little demand
for those who pass long hours in prayer,
or stagger barefoot across Europe,
ministering to the sick, begging for gruel
and singing. And whose voice is thunderous
enough to be heard above the filibuster
of car alarms and MTV anyway? Good thing
I wear earplugs and my trusty blindfold
at all times. Languid, studied devotion;
the maxim your mind runs circles around
for days; realizations that take lifetimes:
there's just no place for those anymore.
Innocent women wear their nightgowns
out to dinner, having exhausted the armor
of their daytime wardrobes. I,
on the other hand, have all the time
in the world, plus the privacy I require,
because I'm always sleeping.
That's my lament, dilemma, handicap,
and advantage. Certainly, when I trudged
from here to here, with my eyes wide open,
I never had a moment alone,
or for anything that wasn't brand-new,
condensed, and predigested. Then my eyelids
became unbearably heavy. Before that,
just like you, I had no time to consider
the possibilities: whether I was
going to throw a punch to defend myself
when push came to shove and shove escalated
to assault, or just lie back on my slab,
wearing a beatific grin and doing nothing.

I never dreamed there existed sufficient
hollowness in me for the blows to echo.
But I heard the first thud on my flesh
cloning itself again and again in my bones.
Who could have dreamed taking a beating
could be so lulling—rain drumming
on a tin roof, and I, trapped inside,
like the glassblower's breath, imprisoned
within the vessel he's carefully shaping
into a bowl which may someday hold water.

A million years ago the earth grew cold. Iowa was covered by twenty-five hundred feet of ice. No one knows why the glaciers formed and spread, or why they eventually retreated.

I blinked and you were gone.

As a boy, he loved the idea of the ice age. Lumbering woolly mammoths and giant sloths. Outside, a vast white edict erasing the landscape. Inside his head, cave paintings of bison leapt in the firelight, their horns spiraling upward, the tips smoking.

Men on skis came to dig you out. Though they worked all night, they were too late.

Waking every day the frost reasserts itself. Its relentlessness a tedium, a closure. The earth must have looked more familiar when all was water. We don't recognize ourselves amidst this overwhelming winter: static that censors newscasts, cold that burns, incessant dripping as icicles perfect themselves. The night skies are a riot of Chinese silk: bolts of crimson and shadow-blue. The radio crackles faintly.

Medical refuse litters the beaches, spews into the water from a backed up sewer under the pier. Bacteria cavort in the seawater. The weather's gone haywire all over the globe. The more sensitive you are the earlier you'll die. Just hold your breath a little longer, dear.

Once you start this medication, you can't stop. Your life changes. You decide, based on a dearth of information, which force you want to submit to: *nature*, now less maternal than ever, or her idiot son—*modern medicine.*

You make an effort to find some grand design in this blindness. If you can't see well enough anymore to edit your film, perhaps you can still do the music. You set an example.

Lemme outa here.

As a boy, before his mother found out and made him stop, he'd bury the frozen birds he found on the porch after big storms by warming the earth first with his father's blowtorch.

Being human, we can't help attempting to arrange events into patterns—the way a sick man sees faces in the stains on his bedroom ceiling. He names them. Months later, they all converse.

The men in the ice-covered radio station play cards and drink bourbon.

What defense can one mount against an avalanche?

Spotless beakers, pipettes, rows of small cages. Welcome to the lab. Here's the chamber where we run preliminary screenings. Better don these gloves. Why not use two pair, like me? The new man on the night shift nods off over his work, with the radio playing. Its tinny strands of music enter his dream disguised as a dead friend's hair. He had short coarse hair, like a terrier's, pleasantly stiff to the touch. The lab is brightly lit to ward off the backwash of night. Under the table the research assistant's feet twitch spasmodically in his sleep.

A series of blurry black-and-white newsreels flickers on screen. Martian canals overflow their banks. A lake in Africa exhales a cloud of poison gas, killing thousands of villagers on its shores. Venice sinks. Anchorage, Alaska, is leveled by earthquakes. Pompeii is breaded and fried by its volcano. The swamp swallows another sand bar, then coughs up a tiny island. Subzero temperatures paralyze Acapulco. *There have been several ice ages*, a female narrator intones. *The most recent lasted 90,000 years.* A timer goes off and the lab assistant jerks awake. In about the time it takes to drink a glass of water, he remembers where he is.

"This is probably the last time I will write to you . . ."

The rocks applaud. Summers turn short and cool. The world remakes itself without us now.

PILLOW TALK

What's the best way to live
without flinching every minute?
How can you lull yourself to sleep
when the laser disc symphony
isn't music to your ears
because tonight you want
not quicksilver but growls
and hisses? Think of vultures,
hippos, frilled lizards—
the noises they make, or silent
viruses doing aerobics under
microscopes. How does anything
begin? Did you originally kiss
me to quell the dread rising
in your head like carbonation?
"Tiny blades of grass point
skyward with forlorn authority,
toward He that sowed them."
I can't believe that either. Try to
be brave anyway. If the *Titanic*'s
salvageable, then maybe today's
travails will leave a romantic
aftertaste, or provide a roller
coaster of desirable side effects,
like all the best modern medicines.

SLOWLY I OPEN MY EYES
(gangster soliloquy)

While the city sleeps there's this blast of silence that follows the whine of daylight: a defeat that wraps itself around buildings like a python, or one of those blue sheets they bundle corpses up in. *Wanna go for an ambulance ride?* Fragments of the sordid and the quote unquote normal vie for my attention. Hacking coughs and seductive yoo-hoos dangle in the 3 a.m. air. Up on this roof, I smoke cigarettes and wait. I feel like god up here. No kidding. Jerusalem Slim on his final night in the garden. Mr. X., Dr. No., The Invisible Man. All the same guy, different movies. It's a city of delinquents: my disciples. Maybe some bum down below finds one of my stubbed out butts and is delighted. Everybody's looking for something to inhale and something else to empty into. The whole city reels and twinkles at my feet, but the stars aren't impressed. They see it every night. The eighty-year-old elevator operator downstairs snores like he's trying to suck up the Hudson. Humans act as if they're going to stick around forever, but nobody ever does. That's what cracks me up.

He wakes from another dream of his fascist youth, where he lay surrounded by the fruits of his skirmishes: a pile of broken bone china at his head, refugees' jewelry at his feet, heaps of fur coats and boots at his right and left hands. Women of all nationalities lolled nude on hammocks in the next room. But now his fatigue's currency is spent. He must wake, face the day, and relearn, as he does every morning, how all those he loved are now dead or elsewhere. Last night a train derailed. Search teams will probe the snow, and he'll join the rescue effort, wipe his brow at noon and glance heavenward. Even he can appreciate a flash of sunlight exposing two clouds' pink and silver collision, sans casualties. His eyes close. An animal pang: he hasn't eaten today, although there are plenty of crumbs in his pants pocket. He rubs his stubble chin, and opens his mouth, or something opens it for him and part of a phrase from an old folk song falls out. The song, grist from his conscience, betrays him. He's still gagging and wiping his lips when they lead him away.

Driving home to River Heights after a hard day's work on a new mystery, Nancy Drew's dark blue roadster lurches and slows. "A flat, I'll bet." Nancy's hunches are spooky; she's almost always right. The young sleuth pulls onto the gravel shoulder, removes her gloves, places her handbag on the seat beside her. Night is falling. Cunningly attired in a simple two-piece linen sports frock with matching sweater, the girl detective changes the tire easily. Though she doesn't relish the work, she's no shirker, and the convertible is soon repaired. Nancy's pooped, so at first she doesn't notice the short, heavy-set man with a large nose approaching. But nothing escapes Nancy's keen gaze for long. "That fellow acts as if he's being pursued," Nancy notes. Her eyes sparkle with anticipation. Her intuition tells her she may be on the threshold of another mystery! As the man draws closer, Nancy controls her excitement, and speaks in a calm, casual voice: "Sir, may I offer you some assistance?" she asks sincerely.

Even after repairing her car, Nancy looks incredibly clean. Her sports frock is perfectly tailored to her trim figure. The color suits her complexion exactly. The creamy pallor of her skin contrasted with the healthy flush of recent exertion still fresh on her cheeks is very becoming. The stranger's face descending toward hers and his unpleasant breath are the last items to register clearly on the amateur detective's mind as his stout, chapped hands find her sweater clasp. Nancy's miffed when she comes to, lying alone in the road. The culprit's vanished. She notices immediately her purse is gone, and with it, her car keys. Her intuition clicking like a geiger counter, she has a revelation she may have lost more than her compact and billfold to this ruffian, as, with leaden feet, she begins the long walk home.

"The modesty of women is thus seen to be greater than that of men by, roughly speaking, about two inches."

Havelock Ellis, The Psychology of Sex

For several moments the fortune-teller studied Della Street's hands, and then she said, "You work. You have a very important position. No?" "That depends on what you mean by important," Della Street said modestly.

"Modesty. Woman's greatest jewel."

Flaubert, Dictionary of Accepted Ideas

He slipped an arm around her waist and said, "Della, you're a lifesaver." Della Street started to say something, then checked herself.

"Nadine Palmer," Mason said, "had something on her mind. Della, suppose you were going swimming with nothing but your underthings on. What would happen?"
"Me?" she asked.
"You."
She said, "MY underthings are in the mode and somewhat negligible. They are nylon and not designed for concealment when wet. I trust the question is scientific and impersonal."
Mason frowned. "It's scientific and impersonal and puzzling."

"There are certain things which are hidden in order to be shown."

Michel de Montaigne

"I'm inclined to think Nadine Palmer squeezed the surplus water out of her undergarments and pushed them into her purse," Mason said.
"And why swim in the nude?" Della Street inquired.
"That," Mason said, "is something that may concern us very deeply."

"A woman may be naked and yet behave like a lady."

Baelz, Zeitschrift für Ethnologie

Della Street smiled knowingly and made it a point to close her shorthand notebook, and put the cap back on her pen.

————

Night inspiration. Work and rest. There are times when you wish to rest but you do not leave your work, the fortune-teller said. What she does during the light of day and under cover of night. How darkness and liquor give courage:
Della Street opened her purse and took out a small flask of whiskey.
"Where did this come from?" Mason asked.
"Out of my private cellar," Della said. "I figured you might need it. Gosh, Chief, you're soaking wet."
Mason tilted the flask to his lips, then handed it back.
"Better take some Della."
"No, thanks, I'm fine."

Your porcelain skin. Your impeccable form. It's almost as if your father had kept you in a jar all these years. You're unmarred. You have been alone in the world a long time. Your mother died when you were young, and your father, he couldn't bear . . . and this left its impression on you, no? You have been aware that when a woman gives her heart she gives everything. Perhaps you fear . . .
Della Street suddenly jerked her hand away.
"That's plenty of fortune-telling for one night," she said, laughing nervously.

————

The strength of the denial of desire. Permission. The unveiling. Modesty means to defend. Modesty is a beckoning. "Come. Here is the shore you seek." Unravel, unpeel, awaken me.

Mason said, "Forget it. This is no time to be coy. Go into the bathroom if you have to, but I want to see those bruises."

44

To strip someone. To humiliate him.

At first, the baths were so dark that men and women could wash side by side, without recognizing each other except by voice, but as day broke, the light entered from every side.

The bathroom door opened. Mason had a glimpse of Mae Farr in flesh-colored underwear struggling back into her dress. Through the crack in the door, she saw Mason's eyes on her and said, "Do you want to look, Mr. Mason?"

Mason glanced at Della Street. "Any luck?" he asked.

"Lots," she said. "She's been mauled all right."

"No," Mason said to Mae Farr. "Get your dress on."

She undressed him, proceeded to undress herself, and rubbed him all over, the entire operation being performed in a serious manner, and in silence. He remained entirely cold.

Modesty and Abandon as rivals.

The restrained maiden, fettered by inhibition, versus the flaunting broad. Is that what it was like?

The modesty of slang, euphemism, of kidding or fibbing. The modesty of silence. Keeping mum. A gag order. The threat of having one's mouth washed out with soap. The prospect of being subpoenaed.

Apparently Della considered the statement called for no comment.

Names too sacred, dangerous, or intimate to utter. The modest substitution of titles or pet names.

She reached up to take possession of his right hand, caressing it with hers. "You'll be careful, Chief?" she asked.

"As to the utility of modesty, it is the mother of love."

Stendhal, De l'amour

She studied him with eyes that saw deep beneath the surface, seeing those things which only a woman can see in a man with whom she had had a long, intimate association . . .

(This may be noted among savages as well as among civilized women.)

"General symptoms of sexual attraction: turmoil, tremors near the waist, weakness in the limbs, pressure, trembling, warmth, weight or beating in the chest, warm wave from feet upward, quivering of heart, stoppage and then rapid beating of the heart, coldness all over followed by heat, dizziness, tingling of the toes and fingers, numbness, something rising in the throat, smarting of the eyes, singing in ears, prickling sensations of face, and pressure inside head." *Partridge*

The lawyer caught her in his arms as she staggered. "Steady," he told her, holding her close to him.

She smiled sleepily and said, "I'm all pins and needles from my knees down. Gosh, I've been asleep a long time."

He slid an arm around her shoulders while she pillowed her cheek against his coat and closed her eyes.

"Let us suppose modesty reduced to aesthetic discomfort, to a woman's fear of displeasing, or of not seeming beautiful enough.

"Even thus defined, how can modesty avoid being always awake and restless?" *Dugas*, La Pudeur

Della smiled a sleep-drugged, wistful little smile. "You do have a way with women, don't you, Chief?"

"I cannot imagine anything that is more sexually exciting than to observe a person of the opposite sex, who, by external or internal force, is compelled to fight against her physical modesty. The more modest she is the more sexually exciting is the picture she presents."

Hans Menjago, Geschlecht und Gesellschaft

Della said, "How does a lady climb over a barbed wire fence in the presence of two gentlemen?"

"Thus modesty is strictly inculcated on women in order that men may be safeguarded from temptation. The fact was overlooked that modesty itself is a temptation."   *Havelock Ellis*, The Psychology of Sex

"I know," Della said quietly.

Della Street blew a kiss to the ceiling.

FIGUREN

Dolls whose heads are made
of shriveled apples. Born old.
Mannequins whose unblinking
helplessness incites torture.
Figurines who spoke among
themselves when the bedroom
was empty. Effigies that can
see in the dark. Graven images
with grief-eroded cheeks.
Dressmakers' forms who usurp
their mistresses' places;
that one over there, in fact,
is my grandmother. Another
smaller doll hides inside
that big wooden one. The blonde
doll has a spare head under her
skirt. His marionettes all went bald.
And I, in my ignorance, did not
believe the damage this spindly
doll could do, stuck full of pins.

The watchful eye notices it's past your bedtime.
Tick-tock. A hairy hand ushers you into the back seat
of grandpa's limousine. It smells like ether.
The measles shot. The harelipped nurse.
A sign on the wall says "Sweet peas are poison."
Tousled hair. Pill bugs. Tinker-toy.
"Here. Draw some zeros." Drinking straw.
Finish your dinner. You're getting too old
to act like that. Ladies keep getting fat
and having babies. Their white gowns fly up,
their wheelchairs zoom down corridors,
into infinity.

I.

Hand axes, rasps, scrapers, penknife blades,
fingertips, rough tongues. Abstract and concrete
ideas ground down till what's underneath grins through.
It took humanity hundreds of thousands of years
to progress from carved to polished stone.
Burnish = caress. I can't keep my ravenous hands
off you. It all comes back to grasp.
I'm desperate to comprehend and be comprehended . . .
Hey you, statue: always facing sideways,
perpetually en route . . . yes, you, winged bull,
priestess, charioteer; you with the hooves
and flute: please take me with you.

II.

Only our century's safe. No reason to flee
to an earlier time. During the childhood of art,
the adolescence of medicine and beer-making,
our ancestors led brief, circumscribed lives,
and left dim histories chiseled into rockface.
Islands populated by giants, nations of goat-headed men.
We kept turning into animals then, we'd arisen so recently.
Were we horses or did we merely sit astride them?
When the race was young, men's wild reverences
were a necessity which has since been conquered,
like smallpox. We're almost cured of the longing
to bow down to WINGED FIGURE OFFERING POMEGRANATE
BRANCH; WINGED BEING POLLINATING SACRED TREE.
Honeysuckle-leaf motifs make way for shining machines.

III.

"This museum is huge. The marble arches make my head
ache. I hear faint arias. I'm a schoolgirl who's lost track
of her class, during a tour by a docent with a slight
British accent. Here at last is my statue.
How did this sculptor, born eons ago, know
I'd come along this morning?
Dusty light tumbles down from high tiny windows.
The light's like more arias, ones my mother listens
to Sunday afternoon while drying the dishes, voices
trilling and climbing. His face turned toward
an invisible speaker, he raises his right hand
to hush us so he can listen. He's still mighty,
though his nose has broken off.
Because of his dignified, tender expression
and his sanded-blind, all-seeing eyes, I want
to kiss this sandstone man. No one's looking.
So I do. His skin is smooth and cool.
This old hunk of stone seems more human
than my social studies teacher. His chiseled
beard juts from the tip of his chin,
all tight curlicues, like empty snail shells.
I hope he knows everything about me
now that I've kissed him."

CHRISTMAS

Brother and sister kiss, then lie
flat on their backs, while
clouds change shape overhead.
They wonder why they have been
kissing like this. Years go by.
They lose track of each other.
The girl takes a job in a hospital
cafeteria, serving meals to night
nurses. She stares out the steamed-
up kitchen window. It's midnight.
Tomorrow's Christmas. The city
lights outshine the stars.
Lately she's afraid to go home.
She thinks her brother will be
sitting on the bottom step
of the stairs leading to her apartment,
eating something, looking up at her
like he knows just what she wants him
to do.

He touches her right breast.
She turns fierce. If he fondles
the left, she grows melancholy
for years. Slowly she becomes
just one more pale criminal.
How tiresome. Nothing's less
erotic than what he's sure of.
Still, he craves a little certainty
to offset the threat of the lesions
he reads about lately:
those puckered flowers—
the first signal the nervous system
is turning to quicksand.
Men once believed plagues
were inflicted by blasts
of hot air, not unlike the gasps
of her complaint-tainted breath.
If only it were that simple.

THE SEXUALITY OF OBJECTS

1. PERSONAL EFFECTS

Underwear, pillowcases, and handkerchiefs are quickly soiled by human use. This ripens them nicely. Brand-new jeans lack meaning. Profound is the dinginess of the sweatband inside father's hat. Mother's bracelets remain faithful in her absence, still tightly clenching their gems in clawlike settings. I collect old clothes. Only your worn ones. But you disgusted me by washing them so regularly, and constant laundering aged your wardrobe considerably. Fabrics wore thin, further weakened by bleach. Collars frayed. I begged you not to be such a rigid sanitarian—to allow a little dirt to collect on the edges of your shirt cuffs and at the hem of your bath towel, to give the fibers something to hang onto. But you wouldn't listen. Now I have precious little left to finger and sniff.

If you were here, you'd growl, "Stop sniveling. All material things must grow beyond themselves. First objects gather dust for a couple of centuries, then spend the next several decades becoming dust again, preparing to be inhaled into a realm cotton, wood, or metal never enter except as threads, splinters, and shards tiny enough to sift through the proverbial needle's eye. Take good care of my piano and hammer, they'll outlast us both." Well, every item you ever had has outlasted you, from the essential to the useless, regardless of its intentions, including me. The photo album full of small squares of treated paper outlived you, enabling me to kiss your picture, but the acid from my lips is slowly causing the sensitive paper to disintegrate, probably from embarrassment. So I kiss the less delicate handle of your golf club (the putter), and the Oldsmobile's steering wheel, where you gripped it. I kiss the kitchen table where your elbows rested at breakfast, right by the ashtray, and it tastes like Lemon Pledge. I must love what you touched, scouring it for tidbits of you left there. The sponge your mother scrubbed you almost raw with in the bath when you were a toddler still remembers you. That stain on the sea-green brocade of the chair by the living room window remembers you well. Your black gloves still revere you by mimicking with their shape the shape of your hands: those small, pert fingers. I depend on them now, to recall the outline of your vanished hands to mind. Their memory is truer than

54

mine, for you never stretched my leather. Holding one of your gloves gently, trying to grasp your possession without marring it. The left glove doesn't wrinkle or grimace. It submits. How easily I slip into it.

2. MACHINES

> "I have always had a passion for machinery," said Karl,
> following his own train of thought . . .
>
> Franz Kafka, Amerika

A. The X-Ray Machine

Lie down. The ray is soft. It will enter but not hurt you. I can see that you don't believe me. It will not pierce you. It penetrates gently, but with utmost readiness. You won't even feel it. When these rays were first discovered, there was wild excitement among scientists. In certain respects, my rays are akin to lights. A small outpouring beams from this machine. I wear rubber gloves, lead-lined spectacles (the better to see you with, my dear), and a rubber apron so none of the rays I discharge splash on me. Now you're a big girl. Your mother's waiting patiently in the other room for us to finish this business. You're not afraid of a little light shining on you this afternoon, are you? That's all it will feel like. Here, now I can see into you. Your diminutive organs and tissues stand out in shaded relief. I, too, feel a slight relief, seeing deeper. Don't fidget, little girl, or you'll ruin the picture and we'll have to do it again. That's better. Your skeleton reveals itself to me in dark shadows amidst the vaguer, interesting tints of flesh. *Ah, me. That I were a glove upon that hand that I might touch that cheek.* Now I know all about you, what you've been hiding, what you had for breakfast yesterday.

B. The Digging Machine

Via these machines that bore great tunnels into the earth, we rediscover love's archaeology. The last rocks fall away as the machine blasts through. Our only friends, these giant machines, chew through increasingly hard rock: mighty moles at our disposal. England and France are united underground, and we meet in the tunnel. The ceiling drips. Soft waterlogged soil falls gently on our heads. No, I *like* you this way best of all: disheveled, slightly grimy, roughed-up. *Beauty too rich for use, for earth too dear.* Down here, even our brightest ideas are smeared. Such tunnels are never con-structed when there's a reasonable, above-ground option, but for us my love, there simply is none. Don't you find the gigantic turbines, the humming of the power generator, the pumps, pipes, and oscillators here underground with us now erotic?

HOUSEBOUND

When we fuck, stars don't peer down: they can't.
We fornicate indoors, under roofs, under wraps;
far from nature's prying eyes—from the trees'
slight green choreography, wrung from rigid trunks,
that leaves us unmoved. In full view of the shower
head and bookcases, we lick and tickle each other.
Every stick of furniture's a witness. We'd like
to believe our love's a private sentiment, yet
how many couches, cots, and benches have soaked up
some? Lust adheres to objects, becomes a prejudice
instilled in utensils by human use. How can I blind
these Peeping Toms—silence the libidinous whining
of these sipped-from paper cups and used toothbrushes?
I can't. I wait for the outspoken adolescent spoons
to rust and hold their tongues so we can be alone.

No one can blame them for their hue or cry, their metallic jealousy. The ache of silver. Plastic's pang. The anger of glass. We cast and sand them into bowls and plates we guzzle from. Turn graceful organic shapes into another form of our incessant babble. Only rubber remains free of hatred, being too flexible and humble to expect any better treatment.

He thinks: how can his true self find delight amidst this clutter? How can he be expected to think clearly? He rings for the maid and goes out for cigars while she straightens up. He checks his reflection in the tobacconist's slightly concave window, pleased with the illusion he has grown taller and lost weight.

Objects' supreme indifference renders them angelic. See: the embossed paper napkin turns into a butterfly and flits away before the little boy finishes his early birthday dinner. The spoon slithers through his fingers during the picnic and quickly burrows into a grassy mound of earth, hissing.

We used to make glue from worn-out nags like you. The knacker was not known for his compassion when pushing those doomed horses over the threshold, through the flaming hoop from creature to thing. At what exact point did their transformation take place, from proud steed to liquid adhesive?

The shy scissors are hiding and you're scheduled to give haircuts to a famous writer and his wife, in five minutes. But where are your German nickel-plated barber's shears? You're left praying to St. Anthony, recoverer of lost things, while you hear from behind a none-too-steady bookshelf a faint silvery giggling.

Garden benches. How their worn stone lumpen-ness reprimands me, like my grandmother's closed eyes.

The oven yawns. The top cupboard shelf belches. A half-peeled lemon squeals like a piglet, lying disgruntled on a wire shelf in the refrigerator, shriveling.

In myths, in the Bible, it was a curse, or the only escape from a fate worse than death: to be flesh and then be changed into a *thing*. This happened to a few luckless women. One turned into a statue, another a pillar of salt, a third, a tree. What punishment. And what staunch peace.

The privilege of *things*: to be and not to do. To rest and emanate.

That necklace she was buried wearing, the glowing opal. When all her flesh has decayed and re-entered the air, the necklace will be her only placeholder in the grave.

We surround ourselves with purchases, gifts, machines that promise ease, and through ease, longevity. They are our spreading shadows. Goods and services. Labor-saving devices. Handy gadgets. We are portrayed at home among our possessions which orbit us, obedient moons. They run rings round us, test their tether, unable to break free and spin away from our grasps. We, however, move as we choose, even gliding outside the picture plane for a breather, stepping through the frame which was never any more or less than a doorway, for a moment of truce. There. That's better. The weather out here's less familiar, more stimulating, more tolerant, 3-D. I light up, enjoy the comfort of a cigarette. See how the affectionate smoke encircles me. To have something other than just hapless oxygen knocking around in my lungs. Something I put there myself.

The objects we speak and move among: aloof fugitives, utilitarian relics, precious ruins whose fatigue reproaches the hands that constantly erode them. Flyswatter, faucet handle, well-thumbed playing cards. Stones of a fortress. Ancient letter in a dead language, locked up tight in the temperature-controlled display case. An armored helmet catches flashes of indecisive museum light. Blink and the objects in the display case fluctuate. They trade places.

The potent bowl. A conspiracy of papers. Solidarity among knickknacks. Inert, smug, undulating. Their reticence vibrates. What does such mute profundity disclose? Speak to me, one of you. The objects' fettered language, in the throes of erosion, sifts beyond my hearing. Under duress, or torture, they only break, never name names.

Clutter tames, chastises us with its halted action. Goads us to paint still lifes . . . dead landscapes to project ourselves into and then wriggle out of when we tire of held breath and blue faces. The artist shakes the paint chips out of his handkerchief, then cleans his glasses vigorously till even you, distant viewer, are reflected in the surface of his shiny eyepieces.

The lunch siren bewails its fate. The smell of cars' hot crumpled chrome bumpers and the tang of melting tar hangs in the air. A whiff of diesel exhaust serves as anesthetic: an odor which implies escape, farewell. Some love this city. Bridges arch their backs. Bands of vandals, each having recruited at least one frustrated calligrapher, roam, renaming streets. If you cannot read the blank ever-temperate climate, if you miss the snow, if you must touch and be touched, then even the stars won't console you in your solitude, which is littered with counterfeit loves, for you have built your pride from the wrong materials. Your emotion's depicted so clearly in each painting in this museum. Your longing appears as a streak in the upper left-hand corner—a blue-gray plume of engine steam—a beautiful spiraling, hopeless exhalation essential to the composition of the painting, but by no means peaceful.

1.   We're all in the same boat.
Water seeps in. One sister borne
away to a mystic seaport, marries
into a foreign family. They never
lay eyes on each other again. Did
you find separation cruel? No,
I found it beautiful. Under the bridge,
lost objects bob by. Look again.
Rub your eyes. Next time you need
a messenger, please send me.

2.   Say hi to her for me. Fire ashore.
No darkness tonight. Here we lie.
Outside: weak rain. In the kitchen:
lenient tea. She writes to me.
Merciful weather. Flares. Red,
red medicine.

3.   Their strength is to sit cross-
legged and silently vibrate. It seems
easy. Cleaner than the havoc light wreaks
on our deceived retinas. Fear not. You'll
live in his mansion, happy and sad
at the same time; deaf to sirens, frogs,
crickets, and waterbugs all calling you
by your maiden name.

Romance is a world, tiny and curved, reflected in a spoon. Perilous as a clean sheet of paper. Why begin? Why sully and crumple a perfectly good surface? Lots of reasons. Sensuality, need for relief, curiosity. Or it's your mission. You could blame the mating instinct: a squat little god carved from shit-colored wood. NO NO NO. It's not dirty. The plight of desire, a longing to consort, to dally, bend over, lose yourself. . . be rubbed till you're shiny as a new minted utensil. A monogrammed butterknife, modern pattern or heirloom? It's a time of plagues and lapses, rips in the ozone layer's bridal veil. One must take comfort in whatever lap one can. He wanted her to bite him, lightly. She wanted to drink a quart of water and get to bed early. Now that's what I call an exciting date. In the voodoun religion, believers can marry their gods. Some nuns wed Jesus, but they have to cut off all their hair first. He's afraid he'll tangle in it, trip and fall. Be laid low. Get lost. Your face: lovely and rough as a gravestone. I kiss it. I do.

In a more pragmatic age many brides' veils later served as their burying shrouds. After they'd paid their dues to mother nature, they commanded last respects. Wreaths, incense, and satin in crypts. In India, marriage of children is common. An army of those who died young marches through your studio this afternoon to rebuke you for closing your eyes to the fullness of the world. But when they get close enough to read what's written on your forehead, they realize you only did what was necessary. They hurriedly skip outside to bless your car, your mangy lawn, and the silver floss tree which bows down in your front yard.

His waiting room is full of pious heathens and the pastor calls them into his office for counseling, two by two. Once you caressed me in a restaurant by poking me with a fork. In those days, any embrace was a strain. In the picture in this encyclopedia, the oriental bride's headdress looks like a paper boat. The caption says: "Marriage in Japan is a formal, solemn ceremony." O bride, fed and bedded down on a sea of Dexatrim, tea, rice, and quinine, can you guide me? Is the current swift? Is there a bridge? What does this old fraction add up to: you over me? Mr. Numerator on top of Miss Denominator? The two of us divided by a line from a psalm, a differing line of thinking, the thin bloodless line of your lips pressed together. At the end of the service, guests often toss rice or old shoes. You had a close shave, handsome. Almost knocked unconscious by a flying army boot, while your friends continued to converse nonchalantly under a canopy of mosquito netting. You never recognized me darling, but I knew you right away. I know my fate when I see it. But it's bad luck to lay eyes on each other before the appropriate moment. So look away. Even from this distance, and the chasm is widening (the room grows huge), I kiss your old and new wounds. I kiss you. I do.

BZZZZZZ

There's a certain beekeeper I've fallen in love with. His hair smells disheveled and fragrant as chaff. His bees are neither captives nor slaves. They're capricious. I'll follow their example. When he leads me into the cool green woods, I'll soothe and rule him. I'll open to reveal the complicated maze of my patiences, stored up since I was a tiny child. Beekeepers constitute a brotherhood. Their urine smells of pinenuts and justice. Each keeper is kept with his head in a cloud like a choirloft. Nectar-fed music is disclosed to him, coded in so many notes he feels handfuls of soot are being thrown in his face and he blinks like a simpleton. But soon the bees mold their keepers into sharp-eyed disciples. Honeybees swarm but cannot be sent out on missions. They dance and form first an anvil, then a breastplate of chain mail, then tornadoes and ancient sayings in the air. At last they serve as my wreath and veil. My love harvests their collective spirit made syrup. He bows to the murmured vernacular of pollen and wax. The sonata hovering over his head, that constant hum, is his promise to me: he'll bind us together with wild zigzag stitches and stings, since nothing but the bees can keep him.

He had treated her gently once before, and she turned to him now
for reassurance: "Maître Pierre, where shall I be tonight?" And on
his asking her if she did not trust in God, she replied that she did,
and that, God willing, she would be in Paradise.
                                    Vita Sackville-West, Saint Joan of Arc

Freed of the harrowing sunlight.
Disinfected. Sundered and spent.
Partially charred. Scattered
to the winds, in a reverie
of prodigies and blemishes.
Handfed by god, or to him.
She died guileless as a choir
of treefrogs, a virgin presiding
over the prickly marriage
of nettles to lilies.

At this point the inconsolable
narrator takes over and finishes
the story in French. He begins
by berating himself
for having found his tongue
a day too late.
Illegitimate child, he cries,
hitting himself in the chest,
stool pigeon, lizard tamer,
granite imp beginning to mold
in the stonemason's basement.
Then he calls out to her,
on his knees in an azure field—
his stricken grin composing
its own pitiful lingo,

that moves you, dear reader,
to tears; right out of your seat
and back in time, to forgive him
for having made the grave mistake
of being neither boy nor girl
to her, before her name was called
and she disappeared from history.
You, reader, are pardoner.

A shadow falls across the lap of a quiet-faced man who's been sharpening pencils, crumpling paper, twitching and mumbling a blue streak all afternoon. The shadow's cool shuts him up. During this moment of truce, as he traces circles in the dust on his desktop, curving endlessly around their empty centers, a certain image invariably springs to his mind. He's a little embarrassed. His thought's a cliché: white calendar pages that curl and are torn away in rapid succession by some indoor windstorm. This moment's hard on him. Fear of waiting, of the jailer's jingling keys, muted sounds growing louder, approaching down the long hall. Fear of the shadow that drives the light away. Ideas hurl themselves into his face like dirty words, and he'd like to lie down in some ritual position, facing east, to receive them. The phone rings. The interruption is brief. He returns to the picture he's trying to remember or visualize for the first time.

The setting is the great outdoors, amidst familiar rolling hills—actually bumps on the back of his father's head under his crew cut. The mood is a tense sobriety that tinkles like glass chimes in an evening breeze, giving its hiding-place away—a tender clarity, ever-fearful of backsliding into blind drunkenness again. He stares out the window. Eucalyptus leaves spiral onto the driveway. The time is back when he was poor and happier; before all his plans boomeranged. The conflict is that all the characters are trying to teach each other a well-deserved lesson. The theme is still up for grabs. But no one cares a fig for any of these dramatic elements, he thinks, except the setting. Pray it's exotic. *Transport us*, we plead, to where we ought to be. We want a rocky island—rocky but tropical, small enough to stroll around in half a day, before the tide comes in. We want pig sties, rows of hard dormitory beds with iron railings, bayous, seedy trailer parks, public aquariums, mine fields. Stuck in the geographical midst of the big picture that looms in his head when he sits down to write, he becomes dizzy, top-heavy, and needs a cigarette. He's a surveyor, who, after gazing about the landscape with a look of terror on his face, plunges his tripod into the earth, and shouts, "Here."

Outdoors, one season was leaving and another was gathering strength. It was autumn, and many days resembled landscape paintings—wild, riled-up clouds, dramatic light. Trees still bloomed but were humbling themselves. Sometimes I felt I had a smirk pasted on my face, being somewhat unused to smiling and to having someone watching me smile. I tried to keep my expression in check.

We'd been friends since we were little. When I thought I might have a chance with him, just for a short time, before he went away, there were a few things I suddenly wanted him to let me do. Some were basic moves, pretty mundane . . . for instance, I wanted him to let me undress him. I wanted to see what his body looked like, and the way different days and moods changed its looks. I wanted to kneel on the floor in front of him and have him stand and rest his hands on the top of my head. Don't ask me why in the world I wanted that. I am not normally desirous of subservient positions. Some of these ideas came directly from dreams. I'd dream about him being in a certain room, with his back to me, about to turn around, and I wanted to be with him in that room, in real life, and I'd be willing to travel to find it, and see if the furniture in the room liked him as much as I did, and how it held his weight. Then my idea that he and I both needed to be human evaporated, and instead I'd wish to be a piece of furniture in that room he occupied, not worried about whether I looked silly or pleasing to him, just cupping his elbows with my armrests, as his flanks and back sank into me.

I wanted to lie with him in the just-cut grass by the filling station, that vacant lot which buzzes and smells fertile and dry. Then the smell of him, of his clothes, of clover; bugs and daylight would seep up to our faces, and I wouldn't know in any given moment which scent to let take control of me. I'd try to see if I could really experience two sensations at once. I wanted him to sit down so I could sit on his lap facing him and wrap my legs around his hips. Then he'd be my folding chair. When I kissed him, my thoughts seemed to be doing a lot of rapid zigzagging. He'd find a place on my neck where it was excruciating, amazing—any pressure or touch and I'd lose my breath, and immediately want to hunt for such a place on his neck, and also not want to move, just close my eyes and let him find other places. When I tried to read what he felt during those sessions, to see what he'd like next, or if he was having a good time, my touch became grasping, motherly, exacting, heavy with an odd attentiveness that disrupted things some. I wanted to touch him much more easily. There are only so many physical movements, and so many ways to receive them. Sometimes I didn't know what to do first, or I was afraid I'd die of terror in the lulls . . . so many risings and fallings when your concentration wavers or focuses and you want someone more or less . . . or you want them not to stop . . . or you want to be alone to think about them without the distraction of their swallowing and breath. So there were waves of warmth and excitement and strong comfort, and slow moments when I thought I might fall asleep, leaning on him, just for a couple of minutes. Then there were moments when I thought: I like this too much, I want it to be over.

Much of this took place in public: in coffee shops, parks, even one time in the library, because we were kids with no place of our own to go. So one minute I'd be swimming in a kiss, rubbing the back of his legs though it wasn't cold—one minute overcome, and the next second rocks of shyness would crop up. I'd feel an embarrassed need to turn my head to see if anyone was watching us. Then another fifteen seconds would pass and there'd be a plateau, or a clearing, in which I'd think: Fuck being in public. Who cares. I wish he'd take his clothes off right now. Then more chagrin, and the sensation we were being stared at—as uncomfortable as when some creepy stranger begins reading over your shoulder on the bus. Then, I'd hit one level higher. The coffee shop would dim, and he'd fill the screen entirely, so I'd be unaware for a few minutes that the waitress had quietly set the bill in its little plastic tray on our table.

RUSSIAN DUSK

When you drink this wine,
which smells of fresh-cut hay,
the moon rises, chaperoned
by the aroma of coal smoke.
The stars flash like the silver
filled molars of my delightful
Lithuanian milkmaid.
Here, take another swig.
Blue evening light, cold darkness.
Shaggy horses exhale steam.
Partial gloom inside the unlit church.
A rooster crowed, a calf bawled
for milk, a dog barked and then
she loosened her babushka
and fell into my arms, knocking
over a chair in her haste
to embrace me.

Hush. Here workers and children come first.
So why should you cry?
Our people produced the first human
to orbit the earth. Typical earthlings,
we love natural grandeur and machines equally,
and can't decide between helicopters and caviar,
trained bears and giant turbines.
Our autumns are soft.
We learn early we're just dots
seen from a great height.
I know you're too excited to sleep.
All newborns are little dictators.
But growing up means being humbled. You'll see.
Be quiet and I'll list some of what
you've got to look forward to. Here,
as in Europe, young girls hold hands
in public. I don't know why I'm so fond
of that sight. Black bread
and circuses are highly recommended,
as are reindeer milk and our Cyrillic alphabet.
The Neva's a beautiful river. White birch bark
the ancients used for paper litters its banks.
Now pipe down. We already have too much
percussion in this life, and as you'll soon learn,
never enough privacy or silence.

ASTRONOMY

When the moon's invisible, do those of us scampering
around down on earth resemble evangelists, or mincemeat?
Do the whitened bodies of women you've loved bleach
in a pit in the clearing, or are they catapulted aloft,
their smoldering fragments lodging in the night canopy,
forming a mosaic akin to a constellation?
After 4,000 years of mystic tradition,
the invention of water clocks, shadow clocks,
sun clocks, and the engraved scale of hours,
human confusion still reaches dizzying heights
well before February (leap year provides little relief),
but at least the spheres hum their colorful mumbo-jumbo
quietly enough not to dismay their neighbors;
at least some of us are still sufficiently naive—
believing our homes to be the center of the universe—
and at least sound waves, channeled through the right
vocal folds, will still elicit tears, as in
"A sigh is still a sigh. . . ," a line from
the song "As Time Goes By."

LIGHTNESS

After the failures of whale oil,
or as a consequence of electricity's
death, weightless days came.
Puddles flashed as we drove through them.
Here's where the sadness dribbles in.
Nothing I dream up can replace the hold
your most holy inattention had on me.
Though mesmerized, I'm floating away.
All that remains is to christen
our dark blue futures.
Tonight, we sit mute in the parked car.
The equation is made. Just this once,
let the absence of readable feeling
(*her truer colors, his heart on his
sleeve*) stand for an immensity of
emotion, too oceanic for show.

OFTEN

You frighten me. Your moods
unnerve me. Your hours get in
my way. At times, when you're
here, and your jacket's tossed
on the floor and there's a half
drunk mug of cold tea in nearly
every room, I decide I just want
to be alone, so I can collect my
thoughts, get up early and work,
without your wants and rhythms
tripping up mine. This morning
I woke to a neighbor's new rooster
crowing. I turned my head and there
was your strange gaunt face at close
range. Icy joy invaded me: you'd
lived through the night. I had to
shove my pillows on the floor
to get a better look at you.

A LOVE POEM

Me Jerusalem, you Kansas City.
You fifth, me jigger.
Me fork, you can opener.
You sweetmeat, me bean-cake.
Me zilch, you nada.

BEFORE SEX

This writhing and thrusting's designed to distract us
from brooding about death. But who can forget
that *all we prize is but lent to us*, anyway:
the length of our days, our contracting attention spans,
the world spun around us and the universe pulsing within.
The penis, the liver, errant patches of hair—
the spirit housed in its aching meat.
Let all flesh bless the stumbling numbered breaths,
the urges. The bloody smells. Long afternoons
in foreign hotels. A premonition of children.
Let those who sleep in the dust guffaw at our antics,
or just lie silent as our half-lives elapse.
We bed down and rise up as often as we can.
Fireflies encircled her head
as she stood on the porch at twilight.
Only this act is real. Only her. Only me.

You appear in a tinny, nickel-and-dime light. The light of turned milk and gloved insults. It could be a gray light you're bathed in; at any rate, it isn't quite white. It's possible you show up coated with a finite layer of the dust that rubs off moths' wings onto kids' grubby fingers. Or you arrive cloaked in a toothache's smoldering glow. Or you stand wrapped like a maypole in rumpled streamers of light torn from threadbare bedsheets. Your gaze flickers like a silent film. You make me lose track. Which dim, deluded light did I last see you in? The light of extinction, most likely, where there are no more primitive tribesmen who worship clumps of human hair. No more roads that turn into snakes, or ribbons. There's no nightlife or lion's share, none of the black-and-red roulette wheels of methedrine that would-be seers like me dream of. You alone exist: eyes like locomotives. A terrible succession of images buffets you: human faces pile up in your sight, like heaps of some flunky's smudged, undone paperwork.

OVERCOME

Few realize this glittering
hour exists. But you do.
The sky molten, the clouds so aroused
they remind you of your mission:
to huff and puff and blow down
the old forms, then erect new altars
from mud, breadcrumbs, and pollen.
Your course, shooting star,
becomes clear for a minute.
The day begins to warm up. What's distant
from us is perfected, I guess. A wind
from the abyss ruffles your hair.
The air thickens into your body
as you move through it.
You never believed a word I said.
Nor were my hands of much use.
My love for you so akin
to homesickness, that tonight,
instead of clouds, the sky looks full
of crumpled bandages and blindfolds.

THE NATURE OF SUFFERING

We know so little about what matters,
what lasts, what constitutes virtue,
what defiles logic by being steeped
in feeling. It's impossible to keep
oneself clean. Every thought
is lecherous and dispensable.
I know I'm not worth the gunpowder
it'd take to blow me to limbo.
You've said so, so often.
Still, I can't leave.
One couldn't trudge far through
this bone-chilling melancholy,
I don't care how impressive
or fur-lined your credentials.
Seclusion produces peculiar symptoms.
A slumbering priestess suffers convulsions.
She's you, trying to shake off
the world's grip, even in her sleep.
What am I to make of her glacial smile?
Outward evidence of voluptuous suffering?
The kiss that's been so long in coming,
rumbling up from her erotic depths?
I found her in a pitiable condition,
much disfigured, but she had already
chosen her road. Every step one takes
is a kind of violation. If I'm
permitted to continue, I must give up
everything. I must be bled white.

Design by David Bullen
Typeset in Mergenthaler Sabon
by Wilsted & Taylor
Printed by Maple-Vail
on acid-free paper